THE
TALKING
CLOTH

A Richard Jackson Book

THE
TALKING
CLOTH

STORY AND
PICTURES BY
**Rhonda
Mitchell**

ORCHARD BOOKS

NEW YORK

Orchard Books, an imprint of Scholastic Inc.
95 Madison Avenue, New York, NY 10016

Manufactured in the United States of America
Printed and bound by Phoenix Color Corp.
Book design by Jennifer Campbell
The text of this book is set in 18 point Garamond Book.
The illustrations are oil on canvas reproduced in full color.

Hardcover 2 3 4 5 6 7 8 9 10
Paperback 1 2 3 4 5 6 7 8 9 10

Library of Congress Cataloging-in-Publication Data
Mitchell, Rhonda.
The talking cloth / story and pictures by Rhonda Mitchell.
p. cm.
"A Richard Jackson book"—Half t.p.
Summary: When Amber and her father go to visit her Aunt Phoebe,
she wraps herself in cloth from Ghana and learns the significance of the
colors and symbols to the Ashanti people.
ISBN 0-531-30004-8 (trade : alk. paper)
ISBN 0-531-33004-4 (lib. bdg. : alk. paper)
ISBN 0-531-07182-0 (pbk. : alk. paper)
[1. Ashanti (African people)—Fiction. 2. Self-esteem—Fiction.
3. Family life—Fiction.] I. Title.
PZ7.M6944Tal 1997 [E]—dc20 96-42152

To Mercedes,
whose daddy is my brother

Aunt Phoebe has things.
Things and things and things.

"A collector of life," Mom calls her.

Daddy says she lives in a junk pile.

"Reminds me of your room, Amber," he says.

I like visiting Aunt Phoebe.

There's no place in her house to be bored,

and she always gives me mocha to drink.

Daddy says it will stunt my growth.

Aunt Phoebe tells him, "Mocha is named

after a city in Yemen, and this child

just grew an inch or two, *inside*, for knowing that."

Aunt Phoebe knows things. . . .

She tells me stories, about her "collection of life,"
each time we visit.
I sip hot mocha and listen, imagining
all the people and places she has seen.

Today we sit in her kitchen and she tells
about the basket of folded cloths in the corner.
"I bought these in Africa," she says.

Daddy laughs. "I figured that was
laundry you hadn't put away."

Aunt Phoebe smiles and takes a cloth
from the top of the basket.
She unfolds it with a flourish—a long magic carpet.
It runs like a white river across the floor.

"What do you do with such a long cloth?" I ask.

"You wear it," says Aunt Phoebe.

"It tells how you are feeling. This cloth talks."

"How can it do that?"

"By its color and what the symbols mean,"
Aunt Phoebe tells me.

"This is *adinkra* cloth from Ghana.
It's made by the Ashanti people and at one time
only royalty wore it," she says.

Aunt Phoebe rubs the cloth against my face.

It's silk and feels smooth.

I imagine myself an Ashanti princess. . . .

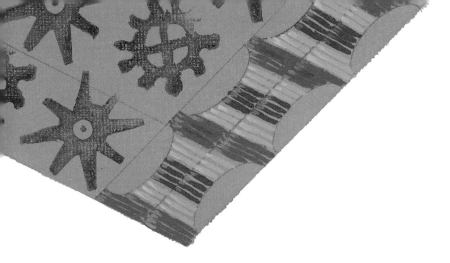

The cloth is embroidered in sections
and hand printed all over with small black symbols.
Like words.
A white cloth means joy—yellow, gold or riches.
Green stands for newness and growth.
Blue is a sign of love, but red is worn only for sad times,
like funerals or during wars.

"Maybe I should wear red
when your daddy comes to visit," Aunt Phoebe says.
Daddy laughs and pours himself some mocha.
He likes to listen too. I know it.

Aunt Phoebe tells the meaning
of some symbols on her cloth.
One says, "Except God I fear none."
That's called *Gye Nyame*.

Another is called *Obi nka Obie.*
"I offend no one without cause."
Each symbol speaks of something different,
like faith, power, or love.

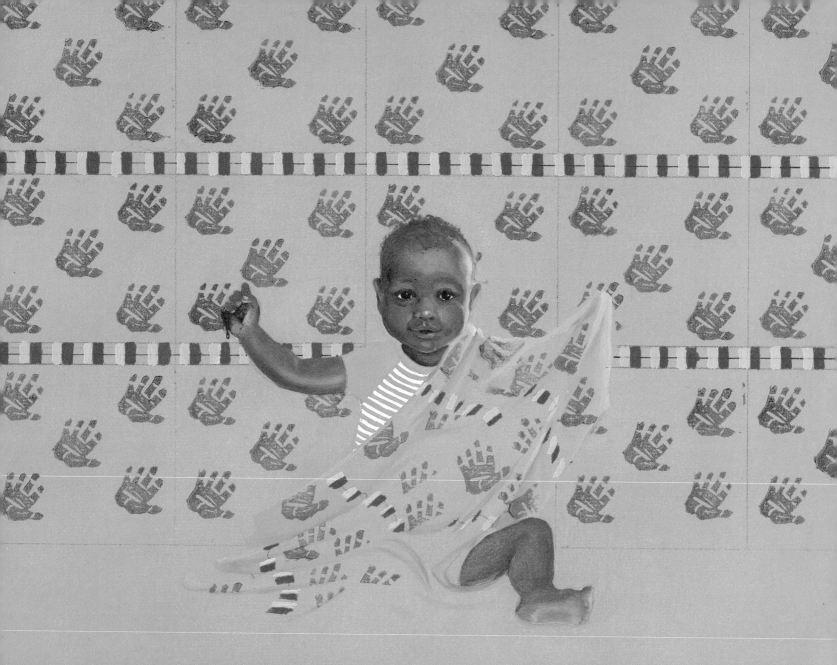

I imagine cloths with my own symbols on them.
Fred—he's my little brother—
should be dressed in green for "go"
with grubby little handprints all over.
Everyone can see what kind of a mess that kid is.

Aunt Phoebe's little brother is my daddy.
"Let's see," she says. "Guess we could wrap him
in gray pinstripe cloth for seriousness, with squares on it!"
We all laugh, imagining that.

I ask if I can put on the *adinkra* cloth.

"Of course you can, baby," Aunt Phoebe says.

"When you're older, you can have it for your own."

She wraps the *adinkra* three times around my waist,

then across one shoulder—

and still it drags on the ground.

"A cloth this long is a sign of wealth," she tells me.

Daddy says, "Amber, you'll need to drink a lot of mocha

to grow tall enough."

"Well," says Aunt Phoebe, "this child has grown a lot,

inside, just today!"

I smile, thinking of it. This cloth means joy.
I am an Ashanti princess now, and here is all my family
and everyone who has ever worn an *adinkra* . . .

gathered around me.